T0157665

PINK INSANITY

JAMAL HOWARD

Order this book online at www.trafford.com
or email orders@trafford.com

Most Trafford titles are also available at major online book retailers.

Printed in the United States of America.

ISBN: 978-1-4669-9682-3 (sc)
ISBN: 978-1-4669-9681-6 (e)

Trafford rev. 06/14/2013

 www.trafford.com

North America & international
toll-free: 1 888 232 4444 (USA & Canada)
phone: 250 383 6864 ♦ fax: 812 355 4082

DEDICATION

I want to Dedicate this Crazy piece of work to my mother Sally Howard, who beat my ass ferociously just to keep me inline. I got the type of ass beatings where you had to strip down naked, with an extension chord tearing your behind up.. It was just like yesterday, me running all thru the house and under furniture trying to escape my Mom's wrath. People today, say that this is child abuse. However, I strongly believe that kids of today could benefit from this type of discipline. Social scientist of today will point out how past forms of discipline, only makes kids more angry... But the jailhouse numbers and lack of productivity tells different. Thank you mom for beating the shit out of me in order to make a better man. For those who read this dedication, may you whip your child's ass to make him a better lover, father and productive member of society...

CONTENTS

ACKNOWLEDGEMENT

I would like to acknowledge 2 spirits.. First I want to give madd credit to the spirit of hard times.. Hard times will make a man out of your punk know it all ass. Hard times will build tenacity and character. If not for hard times, my ass would be weak and still making excuses about what I can not do, instead of what a brother can do.. Next I'll give credit to the spirit of idea and those in their own way who've helped me to bring this book into existence. People are going back to school, becoming entrapaneurs, and making their dreams come true or atleast attempting. It will fuck with your mind seeing all those around you do the damn thing, and your life is stagnant! However, when you come from under the blanket of excuse, you recognize your talent and will even blow up a building to make it happen.. I have taken the best information from all those I associate with, including those who I do not like.. I remember my Uncle Curt telling me that a man figures out how to do things, and not wait on others.. Shit, Money is an obstacle for us all, but it wasn't going to stop me from getting this book published! I also want to give acknoledgement to all those who made me feel stupid. Yes, my job performance may have sucked. Sometimes it isn't that you lack intelligence to do something, but often your intelligence is far to vast for the task at hand! GOD is moving me in a direction more worthy of my existence.. Praise HIM... Praise HIM... I grew up in York, Pennsylvania and that means something to me!! There is no way that I could ever forget those who inspired my Humor in that city. Mike Eccles you were just too damn funny. Your crazy ass and a whole lot others made my childhood the best!! Cracking Jokes on one another in the small town of York was the norm.. At times it got out of hand, still our culture of "cuttin"(our word for cracking jokes) on eachother influenced this ridiculous, yet hilarious peice of work..

CHAPTER 1
Mowanda

Am I a radical or a retard? By day, I own and operate a black power organization. By night, I screw big white women. Times are crucial in the hood, so sisters flocked toward my organization to enroll their sons. Many of the asses attached to these mothers were unbelievable! A black woman's booty is truly a gift for the sighted man and a huge disappointment for the niggas who can't see! During enrollment, I would introduce myself as Mr. Chocolate. Afterward, I would tell them that my last name was Orgasm. You may say that this pick-up line is rather corny, but it went over very well with the sisters. Life is hard and super stressful these days; now name me one woman in her sexual peak who doesn't want an orgasm in these perilous times? I think flirting is good for business and also good for Peter (penis). Every man has a name for his dick, believe it or not. Being that I am a conscious black man, I'm in the process of losing the slave name Peter and renaming my dick Mutombo or Kunta Kinte. I strongly believe that in order to enjoy work, one must mix business with pleasure, so screwing the clientele was necessary. Every day mothers would inquire about the progress of their children. My organization has a no-child-left-behind policy. This means you'll see a difference in behavior and attitude if you agree to my contract allowing me to whip your son's ass. One time a mother approached me in severe anguish about her son wearing his pants hanging off the butt. After about a month in my organization, he no longer reveals his boxers and ass crack. Now the young man walks with a switch, carries a pocketbook, and wears a cheap dress from the Family Dollar. What can I say? Results will vary with each young brother. Chasing pussy was the greatest perk of my job. On the average, I'd screw at least four mothers a year. In 2008, a brother managed to fuck over ten different women. That was a very good year. Good thing for me that the women were all desperate. For some reason, many sisters took their sons out of my organization after we had sex, maybe because they found out that I was a minute man. Getting upset truly baffled me since I gave them the best minute of their life. One day my lust got the better of me. There was this purple-black sister named Zoowanda, who fell for my charm hook, line, and sinker. She had the kind of booty that will put a full moon to shame, and of course, the kid had to have that! After laying down my chocolate charm, she gave up the seven digits with no problem. Giving me her number was rather difficult at first because I couldn't find a writing tool in the entire building; therefore, a brother was forced to scratch the number into my ashy-ass arm. Over the phone, I convinced her that destiny is pulling us together and that we both should go out for dinner at

McDonald's. In my opinion, McDonald's is a classy place with the right company. Plus a brother is constantly broke, so I must be cheap. A date with me might sound tacky, but the dollar menu has a fabulous selection. At the register, the bill totaled up to be six dollars. A brother wasn't paying all that loot, so I asked her to split the tab. Can you believe that the sister copped an attitude? I am taking you out, spending my hard-earned money, and now you want to trip? As Zoowanda stormed out the door, I tried to explain that seven payday loan institutions were garnishing my wages. Of course, she wasn't trying to hear all that, so I started singing "Endless Love" by Lionel Richie and Diana Ross. Women are always suckers for a nigga that can sing. Plus I couldn't let that juicy ass slip away. When she heard the sweet sounds of my voice, Zoowanda resisted no longer and gladly accepted my cheeseburger. What started out as a disaster date ended up going smooth like a baby's ass. We talked about everything imaginable from Popsicles to old cartoons. Zoowanda revealed to me that as a child she had the biggest crush on Papa Smurf. Even to this very day, watching the Smurfs made her wet. From our conversation, I knew homegirl was the inspiration behind the song titled "Super Freak." A dinner date is never complete without a motion picture, so I drove to the hood then purchased a few bootleg movies. Why go to the theater? My plan was to put the moves on Zoowanda while watching TV and then later sell the bootleg copies to her seven kids. I wanted to recoup my money and make a profit at the same time. What can a nigga say? A brother has that entrepreneurial spirit. As we watched the tube, I tried to put my arms around Zoowanda, but she scooted away. When all else fails, dig deep into your playa intellect. One thing about being a pack rat is you never throw a damn thing away. So I went into the closet and found my old VCR player. Afterward, I called my roll dawg Skeeter, who is forty-four, living at home, still a college student for the last twenty years, and still undecided about his major. Skeeter is a good dude despite all his faults. The brother suffers from the Peter Pan syndrome. He just doesn't want to grow up. Every now and then, I let him crash at my crib when his mother throws him out for not cleaning his side of the room in their one-bedroom apartment. Like myself, Skeeter never threw shit away. I just knew he had an old VCR cassette of the Smurfs. Skeeter rode a three-wheel bicycle, so bringing the cassette over was going to take a bit. A brother had to keep Zoowanda entertained while waiting for Skeeter, so I convinced her to let me suck on her toes. After she gave me the go-ahead, I ran upstairs to get the Icy Hot muscle cream as a substitute for Emotion Lotion. Sucking her stubby toes drove her wild. Homegirl couldn't believe that I could deep-throat a foot. Zoowanda screamed, "STOP, THIS IS OUR FIRST

DATE." So a brother respected her wishes. Thirty-five minutes had already gone by, and still no Skeeter. Keeping Zoowanda entertained was proving to be a difficult matter since she didn't like any of the movies. My aim was to get Zoowanda frisky as hell, so I spiked her Kool-Aid with gin. After a few glasses, she began to let loose and tell me some hurting issues, like how her twenty-two-year-old son won't become a man and how she still breast-feeds him every night. Since she was being open about things, I then revealed cheating on my AIDS test and getting a "C." Finally, Skeeter showed up with the tape. Being a good friend, I tipped him a quarter then told him not to spend it all in one place. Quickly I hooked up the VCR, then shit got wilder than a motherfucker. Zoowanda started clawing my back like a cat and biting my neck like one hundred mosquitoes when she saw Papa Smurf. This wasn't romantic at all! This was borderline rape! Afterward, she grabbed my penis and pretended like it was a stick shift. Zoowanda pulled and tugged my pecker as though it was a lever to open a door with one million dollars behind it. She screamed out loud, "I AM GOING TO YANK THIS MOTHERFUCKER OFF 'CAUSE A SISTA IS GONNA CUM." I knew right there that a brother had to fight her off, so I started pounding her head with my fist. Abusing women isn't my motive of operation, but I was being assaulted sexually and in risk of losing the family jewels! Beating her head in didn't work! Immediate action had to be taken before a brother goes dickless! Back in my day, I was known as the Mike Tyson of the projects, and now I can't even knock out a chick! Maybe if I had continued to eat my Wheaties, this shit would already be over. When you date like I do, you're educated on many things like *never fuck with a sister's weave.* When I grabbed her fake hair then exposed the naps, Zoowanda reached for her cell then called the cops. Question, why do the police always seem to believe a woman over a dude? Needless to say, I was arrested for domestic violence. Since I'm a black leader in the community, being in jail can ruin a brother's credibility, so I called my extra-large white pudding pie on the side. Big white women are fashionable for black men these days. All throughout the country, you see a Jabba-the-Hut-sized white woman with a nigga. Sorry-ass brothers can spot a needy big white woman from a mile away. It isn't that I'm sorry; she has a kid from a black guy and drops him off at my organization. I ignored the fact that big mama looked like a horror show, but as time went on, she was added to the list of being chopped and screwed. Of course, she posted bailed and even introduced me to an attorney. Later on, I found out that the chump was really her brother-in-law, who watched the drama *Law and Order* and believed that he was the reincarnated Johnnie Cochran. He may have been a basket case, but brother-in-law got my ass off! Since this incident has somewhat ruined my reputation and dealt me a record, I needed to erase my name from the system. The lawyer suggested that I give Zoowanda cash monthly and agree to accept paternity for her youngest child. Months later, when the trial came before the court, the charges were dropped because Zoowanda lied and told the judge it was a misunderstanding. Yes, I am free from an iron vacation, but I'm stuck paying thirteen years of child support for a kid that isn't mine. Add that to all my payday loans and a brother is more broke than a bum!

CHAPTER 2
Midget

All through my childhood, my ambition was to grow up and become a midget. When this did not happen, things took a dark turn for the worse! Every day, I would walk to the nearest McDonald's, climb the pole, then lie on the golden arches. People would gather and try to talk me down, but I'd turn a deaf ear because the altitude gave me peace. My mind would take me into the most profound thoughts while lying on the golden arches. But no matter how hard I thought about things, there was a question that couldn't be answered, like, when you go to a Chinese restaurant, why do all the menus look alike? Birds would shit on me, and little kids threw rocks; still, nothing could bring me down. Eventually, all good things must come to an end; therefore, bribery got my black ass back on the ground. I was one of the few brothers who had their own apartment at age eighteen, so my mom always took her EBT card and filled my refrigerator. Every time I felt the need to climb the golden arches, Mom would go into her bra and pull out the *card*! After that emotional phase was over, a brother became a crackhead. I wasn't just the common, ordinary rock star but a crackhead with a gimmick! Unlike many crack addicts, I didn't go around begging for money. I was a crackhead with the highest dignity. I'd frequent the Salvation Army, take what was needed, then bypass the register. How could this be stealing, especially since all their items were donated? Later on, I would stand on a corner and make a huge profit from my clothing line. Afterward, I would not only buy crack but give the Salvation Army a sizable donation from the sales. In a way, a brother was working for them and helping their cause. A few years later, I became public enemy number 1 by pulling down fire alarms all around town. To this very day, every time a fire alarm is heard, a sense of pride swells in my soul, knowing that a brother can draw a crowd! With thievery and drug addictions, incarceration usually follows. Jail was a definite turning point in my life. How any brother stays on the revolving-door plan in prison is a definite wonder. My first night in the big house, I was confronted by three dudes named Gorilla, Watergate, and Samson. Clearly, one could see that the three were butt pirates, with my rectum being their final destination! The toilet was in the center of the jail cell. Every time a brother needed some tissue, not only did I have to ask one of them, but they offered to wipe my backside. Not once behind bars did I sleep well! Literally, I'd rest with my fist balled up and my ass cheeks so tight that neither Superman or the Hulk could pry them apart. Sometimes being sexy sucks! Things got to where temptation and lust became so great that the three pillow biters engaged in a crap game to see who'd get my booty. As the game went on, I noticed a bottle of maple syrup next to the dice. Vaseline is hard to come by when you're locked up, so inmates must improvise. Talk about a tense moment! I felt like Farrakhan at a Klan rally! The only thing that should be in my ass is shit and maybe a doctor's finger! Yet try explaining that to three sex-starved homosexuals. Pastor Sweet always spoke about the power of prayer, so if there was a better time for divine intervention, let it be now! I just knew that all hope was gone when Watergate and Samson both had me pinned to the floor with Gorilla using his teeth to pull my pants down! Luckily, a guard was strolling by then quickly moved me to another jail cell, which was occupied by two white supremacists. Lady luck was apparently not my friend! This situation was like a doomsday multiple-choice exam, with option 1 being eaten by sharks or option number 2 jumping out of a plane, having no parachute! Of course, I tried to make the best out of another bad situation, but it's hard to be friendly with a cracker that has *nigger killer* tattooed on his arm! For some reason, only one of them harassed me. Days later, I found out that the more quiet cracker was really a Puerto Rican, disguising himself as a member of the New Nazi Party just to save his own ass. At first, the racist son of a bitch refused to call me by my name. Every time he called me boy, anger just pulsated throughout my system! The best way to repair bad race relations is to come clean about your prejudices, so I asked him about his hostility toward black folks. The cracker explained how his best friend, who was a black man, fucked his wife then stole her away. As the story was being told, this cracker started looking more familiar by the minute. Suddenly it dawned on me that this was White Mike from around the way, who was my vanilla homeboy from back in the day. While telling the story, he paused for a brief moment and recognized my face! White Mike beat the shit out of me for introducing his former wife to my rodeo style. Whoever said that white boys couldn't kick ass should've saw the bite marks on my nipples and fractured toe!

CHAPTER 3
Revelation

Sometimes when I get depressed and Xanax won't do, a brother calls up his pastor to visit the bar for communion. I guess you can label Pastor Sweet as one of those liberal preachers. He didn't mind getting pissy drunk with me then laying hands on a sister's cleavage to drive out unholy spirits. Matter of fact, he did most of his missionary work in the strip clubs. Pastor Sweet wanted to show potential members that he was a down-to-earth preacher, who didn't criticize but listened to their pain and suffering. He usually did this in the private room with his zipper down while putting anointing oil on their breasts. Every Sunday he held services in the tent out in his backyard. Actually, it was several trash bags torn open then held up with broken rakes and shovels. His collection plate was a scratched-up, rusty Crock-Pot that he touted in a Wal-Mart shopping cart. I don't like to spread rumors about a man of the cloth, but word has it that Pastor Sweet borrowed the shopping cart five years ago and never returned it. At every service, he would get irate with the one and only member of his congregation for coming up short in the collection. He didn't understand that times are extremely hard, and making the $400 expected Sunday offering was rough for a laid-off worker from the car wash. Unlike many preachers, he didn't prepare sermons in advance. The pastor often ate at Chinese buffets and collected fortune cookies to base his sermons on. For instance, if the cookie was about ways to enhance finances, he would press the congregation for more loot. If the cookie spoke about love, he would interpret that as a vision for all to join a dating site. In testimony, I admitted being lonely and how chasing various women didn't fill a void. It took him several days to reply, but the answer was mind-blowing and beyond reality. Pastor Sweet came to my house—wearing his usual Sunday do-rag, wifebeater, and hung-low jeans—then stood on the hood of my car with his arms wide open. But before any spiritual advice could be given, I had to make a sizable contribution. Thank the heavens that my income tax was there, or else Pastor Sweet would have kept his mouth closed. Just imagine if I had no money! The pastor is known to throw out a price for spiritual advice, then afterward, you pay monthly installments. When one is finished with the payments, all spiritual advice is delivered. After placing my money in the Crock-Pot, Pastor Sweet yelled, "BROTHER, YOU NEED TO ADOPT A WHITE KID AND RAISE HIM TO BE A BLACK MILITANT." Since Obama is in office, with the Tea Party throwing a monkey wrench in his agenda, this advice deserved a loud "Amen!" If the Tea Party could be infiltrated with a wigger (white nigger), then maybe we could have the upper hand. Quickly after this revelation, I called an adoption agency to set up an interview. The excitement was busting my balls in anticipation of one day being a father to a young

Caucasian child. One never knows the history of a kid upon adoption. With my luck, I'd get one that had behavioral problems like Bart Simpson. After about two hours in the waiting room, the counselor called me to the office. I wanted to showcase my love for children off the bat, so I yelled, "GIVE ME A WHITE BOY!" Before anything else, the counselor asked, "Have you ever been incarcerated?" Even though I was the spelling bee champ in my special education class, still the word *incarcerated* baffled me. My best guess suggested that *incarcerated* is the Spanish word for *circumcision*. Clearly, there was a language barrier between me and the counselor, so the agency sent another in for clarification. I explained to the agency that some of my jail time was the result of false imprisonment. My former employer would hand out paychecks right before closing time. Payday always fell on my off days, so a brother had a tendency to oversleep. One night, I was late getting to the job for my paycheck. To make a long story short, I broke into where I worked then stole my check! Shit, a brother had bills to pay. Plus, there was a Shut Off notice from the water company stuck to my door! In an adoption interview, the first meeting is always tense. I wanted to ensure my chances, so I slept with the counselor. Do you know what it is like letting a freaky sixty-year-old hermaphrodite spank your ass with a walking cane? I sacrificed my dignity for the love of a child, and still the answer was HELL TO THE NO!

CHAPTER 4
Extreme Living

Yes, I am an extreme individual. I might just do what is out of the ordinary just to piss a motherfucker off. That is my only logical reason as to why I made it a must to take a shit in my neighbor's backyard. For months, it was bothering me, looking at dog crap on my grass. I wanted to personally approach my neighbor with kindness and rectify the situation, but there was a small problem—that nigga was bigger than Shaq, and fear kept my punk ass from going over there. Normally, I would have taken the issue up with the residential manager in my apartment complex, but I was several months behind on the rent. How in the hell could a tenant complain about dog shit with rent money owed? So out of consideration for my residential manager, I decided to handle things myself. Picture it: Pennsylvania 2012. A young man steps out his apartment to steal the newspaper from the old lady who lives three doors down, with his favorite pink slippers on, then steps in shit from my next-door neighbor's dog. That following night, all I could do is plot out scenarios to kill my neighbor's mutt. In my mind, all I saw was the dog purposely taunting me by letting out huge, gigantic turds in my grass. The final straw came when he shit on my "vegetable garden." *Vegetable garden* is my code word for marijuana. While going through this issue, I'd occasionally watch *Animal Planet*. The program educated me on how animals aren't too much responsible for their behaviors and why pet owners fail in instructing them. In other words, if the dog is nasty, then the pet owner is nasty. After viewing this, a brother became personally embarrassed about holding a grudge against a mutt. Days after more shit was found on my chronic. I then ran back into my apartment and grabbed a roll of toilet tissue. Afterward, I made myself a gin-and-orange-juice drink to take the edge off. When the drink was finished, I fled to my neighbor's backyard, pulled down my pants, then shit all over his cement. I had to teach him a lesson on respect, and there was no better way other than returning the favor. Sometimes you must act like a fool to get results! People watched in disbelief, seeing me take a stand for my natural right to be respected. Every place that I visit, people stop and stare because I'm now a radical. This incident has made me an urban legend, and all I had to do was shit in my neighbor's yard. The city has even declared that the grounds where I took a shit as a historical place! To this day, there is a flagpole located there.

Being that I am the president and only member of the neighborhood watch program, keeping all under close observation is a must. The old dudes in the barbershop would always say that a person learns something new daily. So the mystery question of the hour will be, is the person who lives across the street from me a man or a woman? This shit has been puzzling me ever since the weirdo moved in two months ago. I even broke into his or her mailbox to see what kind of magazines was ordered. The first week, it was *Sports Illustrated*; the week after, *Bridesmaids*. This led to even more confusion, so I decided to give this person a housewarming gift. I went over with some ChapStick and lipstick then asked him or her to choose one. This motherfucker declined my gifts then hugged me for being so welcoming. If the lipstick was chosen, my thoughts would have been more at ease. I totally agree with loving thy neighbor; I just gotta know whether to look at the booty while the neighbor gets in the car or to give a firm handshake that is usually associated with brothers in the hood. Will I ever find out the sex of the person who lives across the street? Let us just say, homeboy or homegirl will be closely investigated for the sake of being nosy.

My sister stayed around me also. I love her dearly and would follow her to hell with a gasoline jacket on. But each and every time she gave me a dinner invite, there was an extreme shock of fear coursing through my veins. My sister loved to cook, but the roaches kept interfering with you enjoying a meal at her crib. Literally, you had to throw food on the floor just to keep the roaches off the table. Sis also kept a can of Raid as a table weight to hold the napkins down because the window fan had a tendency to blow them all over the house. My sister didn't just have German cockroaches but also the kind that are bigger than house slippers. Not only did she have giant-sized roaches, there were roaches of different species that I couldn't explain! Needless to say, when I returned to my home, a brother had to strip then shake his clothes out before entering. I would never spread the fact that my sibling kept a nasty crib, so I absorbed the embarrassment by letting everyone see me naked while walking into my apartment. Not to brag, but my nakedness put a lot of brothers to shame, especially since I had to use a pool-stick cover for a condom!

CHAPTER 5
The Odd Family

My community was the envy of the city. Most people thought that I was stuck-up just because I lived in the upper part of the ghetto. When guests would visit, they were in awe to see my clothes drying over the balcony instead of the kitchen stove. To be honest, I was the golden boy of the neighborhood. Everyone admired me from far and near. But with admiration comes extreme jealousy. One time, some thugs broke into my crib then stole my couch and love seat! What pissed me off the most was, they could have at least left behind the protective covers! It took me hours to cover that furniture with plastic wrap; therefore, it had sentimental value. Later on I found out the identities of the thieves while attending a family reunion after seeing my furniture in a cousin's house. Matter of fact, every time I visited a relative's house, there was something of mine to be seen! At reunions, I would always wonder why the family voted me most generous especially since they never got a penny from me. Now I know the reason. I take that back; a brother is most generous when it comes to family! One time cousin Lisa fell short on cash. The result was her lights and electricity being disconnected. When hearing of this, immediately I went to the dollar store then purchased some candles for her pitiful ass. Since it was the middle of the summer, I even paid a local crackhead to fan her and the kids. Doing special things for family is a love of mine. During Christmas, I'd cut out coupons and send them to several family members since gift cards were too rich for my blood. As a gag one year, I sent cousin Lola a vibrator for her fortieth birthday. Lola was coming out of a divorce and feeling rather dispirited. My aim was to brighten her morale, but that backfired! Lola has an eight-year-old son who dreams of becoming the next American idol. Our whole family is so proud of him for winning all the local talent shows. We know that he will be the next Michael Jackson or Usher. One day at the family cookout, he was asked to sing "I'll be there" by the Jackson 5. Usually, he would use a comb or brush for a make-believe microphone just to get that real-life effect. Don't know how the hell it happened, but little man was singing to his grandmother with the vibrator buzzing in his hand. As the end of the song approached, with the famous verse "Just look over your shoulder, honey," the young man did a spin, then all the batteries dropped out of the vibrator. An hour later, I saw Uncle Lamar stirring his coffee with it.

Uncle Lamar is the eccentric relative who smells like shit. The world's most stinky fart compares nothing to the smell of Uncle Lamar. The nigga in no way believes in using deodorant. He claimed that it causes cancer, and in Africa, they never wore it; therefore, modern brothers should go without. Whenever we saw Uncle Lamar, I and several cousins held him down while one rinsed him with the garden hose. It took the combined strengths of us all because that stinky motherfucker flopped around like a fish out of water. Looking back, the only true family unity we had was washing Uncle Lamar's funky ass! Aunt Brenda was always a barrel of laughs. She had the most beautiful smile one could ever see—minus several teeth, of course. Why is it that people who have no teeth smile like they're doing a toothpaste ad? Auntie had a reputation of violence, which made it impossible for her to have a man. In her youth, her ex-husband would literally beat the black off her! One night, Aunt Brenda decided to get even after he slapped her for not putting enough hot sauce on the collard greens. Later on that night, while that nigga was sleeping, she took a straight razor then cut the bottom of both feet. Brother man jumped up then fell to the floor. While in agonizing pain and without the ability to stand, Aunt Brenda beat that bitch until the cops arrived. Adding insult to injury, Auntie didn't even see one day behind bars. Since the ex-husband was wanted in three states for robbing liquor stores, the authorities dropped all charges and gave her the reward money! The major topic among family has now been "With all that cash, why does Brenda still have no teeth?" We all know that she is desperate, so the money probably went toward buying the affections of young men. Our family isn't one to judge and certainly is not a family of leaving a relative in despair. So at every reunion, we send several of the teenage cousins out on the boulevard and with dark shades, walking canes, and tin cans. In the last three years, we have managed to get five dollars toward Aunt Brenda's teeth. Thank the heavens for charity. And there was Uncle Bernie! He really wasn't my uncle, just a friend of the family who was always around. Bernie provided the family with meat for our cookouts. He would go into the grocery store in the middle of summer with a fur coat on then steal all the bologna and hotdogs. Bernie was a guru at thievery. He's the only nigga I know that could go into Rent-A-Center and come out with a couch underneath his fur coat. My mother hated Bernie with a passion. Every time he got drunk, Bernie told everybody that I was his son. In a way, I kind of believed him. Back in the day, Bernie would go to the corner store and steal birthday cards then deliver them to my school daily. He was the only dad that a brother ever knew, so I made sure his glass of gin stayed full at every family gathering! Uncle Eric was the most dishonest person you could ever know. We all know that the sky is blue, but somehow Uncle Eric could have you believing that it's really green. Like Bernie, Uncle Eric was also a thief. I can remember being a snotty-nose kid back in the day and asking Uncle Eric for a dollar. My loving uncle never hesitated giving me the buck with no questions, then later when I fell asleep, he stole it from my pocket!

Eric was an alcoholic without question. Blacking out was nothing but the usual for him when he was under the influence of that fire water! One time, Eric got so drunk that he climbed into an apartment window while people were sitting and watching TV on their couch. Good ole Unc got the beat down of his life 'cause those people just knew his ass was trying to rob them. Little did anybody know that Uncle Eric lived there three years ago, believing he still did.

CHAPTER 6
In Pursuit

I haven't been able to sleep a wink as of late. For some reason, I keep having dreams about watermelons wearing baby diapers. Pastor Sweet says that my new synthetic-weed addiction is having irreversible side effects, so he advised me to pick up a hobby. Like many niggas, I spend without really having any cash, so I decided to max out my girlfriend's credit card then go on a shopping spree at the Family Dollar! Retail therapy is the greatest hobby that a dude can have. One gets to buy all the shit that isn't really needed, like Carpet Fresh. Even though all my floors are tile, a brother can use it for baby powder. Who will ever know? Plus the scented brands can have a cologne-type smell, which will add to your swag! After about an hour of shopping, I then walked up to the register with five carts full of merchandise. My sex symbol status is always existent, so I butted in front of several women just to let them get a sneak peek of my ass. As the cashier totaled up the merchandise, I noticed that some badass ghetto kids were stealing out of my shopping cart. Being that I am a champion for justice, apprehending these juvenile delinquents became a must. I chased those little bastards around the store for at least fifteen minutes! We knocked down racks of toilet tissue, old ladies, and a Coca-Cola machine.

Eventually, the pursuit led to the streets, with me running like hell and my voice sounding like a police siren! As the chase went on, those juveniles had a nigga jumping over cars like a superhero, and they were much more clever than I originally had thought because they suddenly branched off into two teams of four. Backup was needed immediately, so I called Skeeter since he lived around the corner! Skeeter didn't pick up; therefore, I was forced to leave a message. Hopefully, Skeeter could understand the message 'cause I was breathing and coughing like crazy from running after these little motherfuckers. Approximately two hours after the whole ordeal began, I eventually cornered one of them in a dark alley. My first reaction was to take a wet dish towel then beat his ass senseless, but I just couldn't! That little nigga was shaking in fear, and his eyes were like a fire hydrant. I believe when an adult is talking to children, he or she should have a commanding voice. So I asked this future O. J. Simpson to empty out his pockets! Can you believe that he pulled out a pack of tampons that was stolen from my cart! I asked the little nigga, "Why in the world would a young man steal tampons?" He replied, "I just wanted to get my mom and her girlfriend a nice anniversary gift." My sympathy for this young man rivaled the size of the universe. How in the hell could I put the belt and law on this kid when all he was trying to do was get his momma a gift? After hearing his reasoning, I was forced to let him go. Did I do the proper thing? A week later, I saw this same kid in the newspaper for robbing the local drug dealer of all his cash. When the authorities finally apprehended him, his ass was hiding in a funeral parlor and playing dead in a coffin, wearing a Chicago Bulls jersey with the number 23 and breathing loud enough to blow his cover. Talk about the world's dumbest criminals. I should've whooped his ass!

CHAPTER 7
The Expensive Gift

Not only am I a caring family man, I'm also a protector and confidant to my most trusted friends. Skeeter was always broke, so he tended to borrow money from everyone he came in contact with. He even owed the neighborhood kids! His picture was in every elementary school and with a caption underneath that said, "Wanted: Grown-ass nigga for not paying up." Skeeter had to walk around with dark shades on and a wig whenever he stepped foot out of the house. He was always recognized no matter the disguise because he wore the same clothes every day. Not only would Skeeter borrow the lunch money from grade-schoolers, he would agree to double their return. When this didn't happen, the parents usually got involved and would give him the beat down of his life! Every week Skeeter would have fresh cuts and bruises across his face. I could no longer allow this to go on, especially after getting a call from the emergency room. However, this beat down didn't come from a kid's parent. This ass kicking came from his mother for not paying back rent. When I arrived at the ER, his mother was standing over the bed and threatening that she'd break another leg if he didn't hand over the debit card. Seeing Ms. Molly badgering her own son forced me to get involved. Pastor Sweet often spoke about family unity! Who is a better expert other than him? After all, he was on divorce number 6. When I attempted to teach Ms. Molly some parental skills, she grabbed her cell phone and then called a few church sisters. My first thought was that she wanted a prayer service for her and Skeeter in hopes that they could mend their differences. Instead, the church sisters came in the ER with Bibles and switchblades, threatening me with open-heart surgery if I didn't take my ass home. I mean, what can you expect? They didn't go to Pastor Sweet's church, so how righteous could they be? After Skeeter's release from the hospital, I decided to go gift shopping on the boulevard and purchase him a prostitute. Skeeter is my boy through thick and thin, but most women wouldn't fuck him even if a gun was being held up to their child's head. He was just that homely looking! The nigga didn't have swag. He had yuck and gag! The trick that I picked out for Skeeter was a sight for sore eyes. Indeed, the sister was lovely and hotter than a jalapeño's booty! When Skeeter first laid eyes upon her, he cried in disbelief that a gorgeous woman could ever want him. Unbeknown to him that she was being paid by the hour, the first date I could afford with no problem. However, I didn't count on Skeeter falling in love. I now had a dilemma! With my money drying up and Skeeter expecting to introduce Boom Boom Belinda to his mother this upcoming Saturday night, what was I to do? I could get the cash from Pastor Sweet, but the 100 percent interest rate he charges is far too rich for my blood! Boom Boom Belinda was in no way cheap! At $50 an hour with a five-hour minimum, one could understand my worry. The day finally came when I could no longer purchase love for Skeeter, so a decision had to be made. My sister was in need of a good man, and Skeeter was just the right one! Since Skeeter had a problem with long—and short-term employment, my sister was just the right one because taking care of a sorry-ass nigga was her favorite pastime. At first they seemed to hit it off, but his complaints of her crowding him was the death of their relationship. Before Skeeter moved in with Pastor Sweet, he shared a one-bedroom efficiency with his mother, which is something he enjoyed and often bragged about at the basketball court. So him being crowded was a mystery to me.

CHAPTER 8
The Joy Ride

Some days I like to scoop up the boys and go cruising around the hood. Every man must take a break from his woman in order to fully enjoy life. Don't get me wrong; a woman is a good thing, but they all possess bitch tendencies. I, Skeeter, and Pastor Sweet were all in serious or complicated relationships, so we all went for a short drive. Pastor Sweet informed me that he couldn't be with us all day because on Tuesdays he runs a swimsuit competition in front of the church to raise funds for his alimony payments. As we drove and cruised the never-ending ghetto of Pennsylvania, the pastor began to mentor Skeeter on ways to become a man and get the hell out of his momma's house. The pastor's words were so moving that Skeeter agreed to move in with him and live in the basement for a small fee. Pastor Sweet knew that Skeeter received a check at the end of the month for being bipolar and felt that he was entitled to it! In his famous words, "If blessings don't come your way, then you gotta create your own." Like always, the pastor gave me a lifetime of advice on the dangers of chasing women. Each and every time he gave me a sermon, my life seemed to get better! "Too much of something isn't a good thing" was a common sermon of his, so I made the decision to stop having three women a night! Now I only have two women in my bed at a time. Another sermon that was quite common with the pastor was "change is gradual." Skeeter had an annoying habit of sucking on boiled peanuts then leaving the shells in the backseat of my ride! He and I would argue about respecting the cleanliness of my car, but he just couldn't comprehend anything that was said. Skeeter also had a fast-food addiction that was putting weight on him like crazy. During our drive, Skeeter insisted that we go to Hardee's. The line was long as hell, so we decided to order from the drive-through. This greedy bitch ordered three burgers, two fries, and seven milk shakes all for himself. Did he offer me and the pastor any? No he didn't! While paying for the food at the drive-through window, Skeeter asked if he could have his order to go. Now that's what you call a dumb ass! Shortly after Skeeter opened his mouth, Pastor Sweet said a prayer for him to have the wisdom of Solomon. Other than Skeeter's silly ass, this joyride couldn't get any crazier! Pastor Sweet would constantly change his status from pastor to messiah. Some days the pastor would go on about how he was the Second Coming and had the awesome power to turn water into wine. Seemingly, he only made these claims while coming out of the liquor store with a brown paper bag! Supposedly, he did his miracles in the restroom of the liquor store where no one could see him. I've been told that he purchases his booze at the counter like everybody else, but I refuse to believe it! After about three hours of driving, Pastor Sweet took over the wheel. His claims of messianic powers kept on as he drove the Blazer with no foot on the gas pedal up the highway. His aim was to show Skeeter that all things are possible with faith. Pastor Sweet said faith allowed him to drive with no foot on the pedal. Skeeter later told me that while I was sleeping, the pastor secretly hit the cruise control. Come to think of it, Pastor Sweet also claimed that the doors automatically opened for him at the Wal-Mart entrance, which, according to him, was further proof of his divinity. When Skeeter took over the wheel, it was more like a beginner's course for new drivers. At age forty-four, you'd think that he had a driver's license. Just last month, he finally passed the written test for his permit after taking it for the four hundredth time. Teaching Skeeter how to drive was more of a difficult matter than I had originally thought. I and the pastor spent the first ten minutes trying to explain that the glove compartment and trunk weren't one and the same. Skeeter had no clue on how to use the turning signals. When making a right or left turn, he would yell out of the window to alert other vehicles on which way he was going! All the time that Skeeter drove, I and the pastor found ourselves cautioning him about driving on the sidewalk. Skeeter believed that sidewalks were shortcuts to reaching a desired destination. Even if it meant possibly injuring a pedestrian, he was going to get there by any means necessary! When Skeeter's time was up, I quickly jumped back behind the wheel and drove those two silly niggas back home.

CHAPTER 9
Roommate

Pastor Sweet would always talk about forgiveness, but when it came to Skeeter, his religion was null and void. At first their roommate situation seemed to be working out, with only a few complaints here and there. As time went on, the pastor renamed Skeeter as the Devil's son-in-law. The first of many issues was when Skeeter used Pastor Sweet's anointing oil for cocoa butter. Skeeter didn't understand what privacy meant. On many nights when Pastor Sweet was performing exorcisms (with his many female followers), Skeeter ignored the No Entering sign on the door and interrupted the naked ceremony. Pastor Sweet's reasoning behind nude exorcisms was that evil spirits couldn't exit the body with a person wearing cotton, rayon, or silk. Skeeter also had a bad habit of taking without asking. On several occasions, he'd put on the pastor's underwear when his mother refused to do his laundry. The pastor only had two pairs of drawers, and most of the time, he was out of luck 'cause the shit stains left from Skeeter made his undergarments impossible to wear! Flushing the toilet was another issue with Skeeter. He had a scary childhood experience at sea, so when the toilet needed to be flushed, he would call the pastor on his cell phone from across the hallway then ask him to flush it. Sometimes the pastor was gone weeks at a time due to out-of-town church revivals. After these events, he'd come home to a house that smelled horrible. The beloved pastor was a super neat freak, so when he came home from the tiresome revivals with his house smelling like spoiled chicken, he went postal on Skeeter by hitting him with everything in the house but the kitchen sink. Being around Pastor Sweet had a reverse effect on Skeeter. He thought that the pastor had far too many rules, which caused great stress in his life. Skeeter could easily have gone back to his mother's, but by this time, she now had a live-in boyfriend. When people go through stress and worry, they usually start acting out. Poor Skeeter started hanging with the local thugs for the attention that he wasn't getting at Pastor Sweet's home. An outside influence is always stronger than a domestic one, so it didn't take Skeeter long to adapt to thug life. A typical thug carries a firearm. Skeeter carried a butter knife in his back pocket, with a red scarf wrapped around it. When visiting the pastor's home, I would see Skeeter stabbing at the pet hamster, in practice for a one-day gang fight. The gang fight never came, but the physical quarrel with him and the pastor surely did. The final straw came when the pastor went to dry himself off with his bathroom towel and noticed that it smelled like pure ass. To make extra money on the side, Skeeter would babysit for relatives. A cousin had forgotten to pack diapers, so he was forced to use the pastor's towel.

Baby shit can be a gruesome thing, especially when it gets in the eyes and under the fingernails. The fight lasted for hours! I never knew that a man of the cloth could curse and throw punches without pause! Not only was Skeeter's mom beating the hell out of him, now it was his own pastor! Until then, Skeeter wouldn't fight back even if his life depended on it, but this time, he mustered up the strength to cast out fear. To make a long story short, the pastor was rushed to the emergency room for bite marks on both ankles. After beating up the pastor, Skeeter began to get a swelled head. The brother just knew he was all that and a bowl of chitterlings now that he could finally kick some ass. This new tough-guy persona made him unbearable to be around! Whenever he and I hung out, Skeeter would put me in a wrestling move out of nowhere. He even put a choke hold on my cat! Finally, I had to have a conversation with Skeeter about his abuse of people. I showed him that he was starting to put a wedge on our friendship, so he apologized not only to me but also to the pastor. To my surprise, the pastor didn't accept his apology and demanded that Skeeter find room and board elsewhere! Skeeter was my dawg, so if he needed a place to stay, then no problem! The first night that he stayed in my house was rather crazy! I woke up the next morning with Skeeter's tongue in my navel. He failed to mention about his sleepwalking issue. The second night, he urinated in my kitchen pantry with the belief that it was the bathroom! The final straw came when he failed to rinse the tub out thoroughly from his baby-oil baths, which made me fall and bust my ass! Sadly, like all before me, I threw his bitch ass out of my house! I am quite known for my great diplomacy skills, which will be needed to convince Skeeter's mom to take his trifling ass back in!

CHAPTER 10
The Crazy Raid

Ms. Bishop was a busy lady, and setting up time with her to discuss her son's homeless situation was quite a calculus test. She was totally into her new man, who was very demanding about being pampered. Before this new nigga, she'd spray cologne all over the pillow at bedtime just so it felt like a man was sleeping next to her. Talk about desperate. After work, she'd come home then clip his toenails with her teeth and spit them out on the rug. Whenever guests would visit, they'd have to take a sharp instrument to scrape out the nails from the treads of their shoes. Ms. Bishop now had everything she wanted in a man, so why bring her lazy son back, who didn't hardly contribute? That is what she told me upon my mentioning Skeeter's name. That heifer didn't even give me the time to present a strong argument. Skeeter was running out of options, so now what can be done? I decided to let Skeeter sleep in my backyard and allow him to come in the house only to bathe, eat, and shit. That was a huge mistake! This nigga ended up digging holes all through my lawn so the neighborhood rabbits could have a place to stay. He even tore my charcoal grill apart then turned it into a birdbath. My backyard now looked like a land mine, and on top of it all, my apartment manager wanted cash for the damage! This proved Skeeter to be destructive; therefore, I was forced to put him in a shelter! Could

Skeeter deal with the typical schizophrenic people that usually reside in homeless shelters? At this point, I no longer cared! My life was Skeeter-free, so I thought. About two days later, I heard rocks being thrown at my window. At first, I thought myself to be dreaming about a mass invasion from all those I owed money to. Can you believe that this bitch was outside singing Christmas carols with several residents from the homeless shelter in the middle of July? Right about then, I came to realize what all the others already knew. Skeeter was a special needs *case*! I truly wanted to call the cops, but Skeeter was rumored to carry a pistol. If the police would happen to arrest him carrying a piece, they might want to charge him with every shooting since Abraham Lincoln. The police is hard on niggas from urban areas. I just couldn't do that to my boy. In order to truly be free of Skeeter, I had to succeed where Pastor Sweet failed, by kicking his narrow black ass! I had an old curtain rod hidden in the back of my closet for protection reasons. I grabbed it, rushed outside, and started swinging it at Skeeter and his flunkies from the shelter. All at once, they bum-rushed me then tossed my ass to the middle of the street. Afterward, he and his homeless flunkies ran into my crib then locked me out. They even threw Shabba (my cat) and his litter box out my crib. There I was stretched out on the street, with cat litter all over me! Later that night, I sought the counsel of my beloved pastor for help in this situation. His advice was to pray on it!

CHAPTER 11
Living At The Laundromat

Now where was I to go? Pastor Sweet would take me in without question, but his preachy self-righteous attitude that's usually associated with preachers sometimes got on my nerves. A good-looking nigga such as myself could go stay with one of my honeys, but then I wouldn't be free to go out on dates. I had a cousin who was the attendant at the twenty-four-hour Laundromat. I was quite sure that I could lay my head there for a few days or maybe sleep behind a washer or dryer. The first couple of nights, things were quite uncomfortable sleeping in between two washers with the spin cycle keeping me up periodically through the night. On top of all that, I'd wake up with bleach stains all over my black pajamas with polka dots. My cousin's boss would come in every morning before his shift was over just to see if things were getting done. This meant that I had to have my ass up out of there by 5:00 a.m. One day he caught me sleeping behind the washer. I awoke and quickly played it off like I was the repairman. I started pulling out wires and banging my fist on the washer like something was really wrong with it. He asked me, "Where are your tools?" I said, "In the truck." Afterward, I ran outside then waited for his ass to leave. Living at the Laundromat went on for about a month until one of my honeys wanted a candlelit dinner at home. I took an ironing board, placed a decorative tablecloth over it, then put some flowers on top and made it a table. After that, I found two lawn chairs and placed them on opposite sides of my new table then dragged my new nigga-rigged dining set right to the middle of the Laundromat. With the Laundromat being less busy between the hours of 11:00 p.m. and 1:00 a.m., interruptions would be at a minimum, so I thought. Every time I gazed into her baby-blue eyes, someone would ask me where the change machine was. At first, my date didn't seem bothered, but as the night went on, one could see the annoyance in her face. As our dinner date came to a close, she hinted about coming over to her spot for a nightcap. It didn't take an always-horny brother such as myself long to say *yes!* We fucked like two jackrabbits on energy drinks without pause. In between nuts, I noticed that her cell kept ringing constantly. After a while, it started sounding like chalk on a board with every hump, so eventually, she got up and turned the ringer off. A little later, she went downstairs to get me a soda as a reward for doing such a great job! From downstairs, I could hear her scream, "IF YOU DON'T LEAVE, I'M CALLING THE COPS!" I came to find out that her ex-boyfriend wanted entrance into the house. Finally, she brought my soda up then played it off like I didn't hear a thing. As we laid together, I noticed that this chick was wearing a wig. As I continued to stare, she explained that the hysterectomy took most of her hair out and that, in all honesty, she was really a woman. I never doubted for a second that she wasn't a woman or maybe one of those hermaphrodites. Still, I was very curious as to what this chick looked like without a wig, so I asked her to remove it. Boy, was that a mistake! This girl looked like sin dipped in sorrow! I have never seen so many stitches and staples in a human head in all my life. My first thought was, *Is this bitch machine or woman!* I ain't the brightest nigga in the world, but in no way could a hysterectomy do this! By my facial expression, she could tell that I wanted a more detailed explanation on her appearance. She finally admitted to mixing a few household chemicals together in order to make a homemade perm. The morning was now here, and leaving was the premier thought in my mind! I blew homegirl a kiss then pulled the fuck out of there! While driving off, her ex-nigga kept looking at me like he wanted to start a beef, so I backed my ride up, rolled down the window, and said, "That ugly motherfucker is all yours, and I should kick yo' ass for wanting to wife her."

CHAPTER 12
Seizing My Home

I had finally gotten to the point where I needed to reclaim my home! Word on the street said that Skeeter had turned my home into a registration center for the Special Olympics. I didn't find this hard to believe since Skeeter and his merry band of social rejects could be classified as retarded! Taking my home back was going to be a challenge indeed! My first plan was to frame Skeeter and his boys by calling the cops and stating that they had illegal drug paraphernalia. When the police came to search the premises, all they found was Skeeter sniffing aspirin in its powder form. My second plan was to accuse him of running an illegal dog-fighting ring. When animal services entered the house, all they found were empty cans of dog food in the kitchen sink. Since Skeeter and his flunkies didn't work, they had to feed themselves in the most affordable way. I had tried a million ways to remove Skeeter from my home, and nothing seemed to work! All options had been exhausted; therefore, I was left with the only choice: burn down the house. Burning my crib down didn't seem logical, but with me having rental insurance recouping, the loss wasn't a problem at all. Now how could I set the motherfucker on fire without any suspicion of arson? As you know, Skeeter was a bona fide dumb bitch, and being that he was probably tired of eating puppy chow, I decided to send him a pack of ramen noodles as a peace offering. I instructed him to microwave the noodles in a metal pan for at least thirty minutes. Skeeter did as I knew he would. From afar, I could see not only my crib burning the fuck down, also I could see Skeeter and the boys rolling on the ground to extinguish the fire on their backs. Skeeter walked away with third-degree burns, which was a small price to pay for all the bullshit he put me through. Do I feel bad about Skeeter receiving skin graphs and being slightly disfigured? I felt a whole lot worse sleeping in the Laundromat.

CHAPTER 13
Living At Sweets

I am super thankful to my cousin for letting me rest my head at his place of employment; however, going back to the Laundromat was something I could no longer do. My rental insurance check wouldn't be here for another month, and Pastor Sweet was now the only lifeline that I had. Pastor Sweet made it mandatory to attend his church while you stayed at his place. He also expected you to pay that unreasonable $400 tithe. If you couldn't pay it, he'd put it on the church's tab with interest added. He just knew my insurance money was coming any day now, so he didn't sweat me not paying. Those that couldn't pay, he would send his mystery deacon after them to collect payment, who carried a bat and some rope on his person. Maybe that is the reason why he could only keep one member in his congregation. I loved Pastor Sweet for continually guiding me through hard times, but I now started to question his righteousness, especially since this young lady kept coming to the house night after night, demanding child support payment for her six-month-old baby. I knew that the pastor had children all over town before he was saved. But to have a recently born child out of wedlock and claiming to be a pastor, this will most definitely shatter my faith—if the shit is true, of course. I knew that Sweet performed exorcisms in the privacy of his bedroom, but what I heard didn't sound anything like demons coming out. It sounded more like sex moans with something going in! Quickly I rushed out of bed, broke the door down, and saw the pastor, Skeeter's mom, and my sister doing the grown folk! At that moment, I was frozen like a snowman with disbelief. Not one of them had a damn thing to say except Pastor Sweet. All he could say was "You wanna join in?" No longer could I stay at Pastor Sweet's! My life had taken another turn for the worse 'cause everybody close to me was a basket case. I needed a place to go and get away from it all, so I went back to Pastor Sweet's home and locked myself in his closet. I stayed cooked up in there for three weeks and four days with two gallons of water and a bucket to piss and shit in. As the days went, my life gained more clarity in that dark and moldy closet. I had been led astray by this counterfeit preacher, and his ass needed a lesson much like Skeeter did. To expose this so-called preacher, I went to the local newspaper then informed them on how this pastor was leading the flock astray. That upcoming Sunday, the local news and cameramen poured down on Sweet's congregation like a narcotics unit only to find that Sweet changed his title from messiah and pastor to the Holy Pimp. With this title change, they couldn't expose him as a fraud because he was actually living the life he taught. Sweet was always quick on his toes when it came to nearly being exposed. No matter the case, I am done with this nigga!

CHAPTER 14
Getting The Freak Out

With no Pastor Sweet or Skeeter, my life was beginning to become less complicated. Removing those two boneheads was an easy matter, but I couldn't just cut my sister off. She had now reached hoe status, being that she fucked two of my ex-friends! Since I'm a mack daddy in recovery, there was no reason that my sister couldn't get the freak out of her and become respectable. There is no rehabilitation program for sluts, so I took it upon myself to make her a virtuous woman. I first went into her closet then cut up all the see-through and revealing attire that she owned. After that, I started a nasty rumor around town that she had genital herpes so that nobody would dare fuck her during the rehabilitation process. The first month, I made her walk up and down the stairs and chant "I am somebody." I truly believe that if you say something long enough, one will condition themselves to believe it. She repeated it like a good ole girl with no problems at first. But then after a while, my sister began to say it as though she had Tourette's syndrome. Can you believe that the manager threw us both out of Denny's for her continual outburst? I also made her write in crayon "I am not a garden tool" one hundred times on construction paper then hang it on the refrigerator. After three months of hoe rehabilitation, everyone could see a drastic change in style and behavior. I was so proud that I could stop that family tradition of being a hoe! See, we come from a long line of undercover freaks that stretches way back to medieval times. Everything was going fine and dandy for a while until she ran up to my ass one day while shopping at the Salvation Army with a pregnancy test that revealed positive! All this time I had thought that the weight gain was caused by whore recovery. But the thing that blew my mind the most was finding out that the unborn baby could be either Pastor Sweet's or Skeeter's. Whoever the father might be, the child was sure to be doomed! In addition to all that mayhem, I had made a solemn oath about being done with Sweet and Skeeter; now things were more than complicated! I decided to call a truce with my former dawgs for the baby's sake. I explained to them the seriousness of raising a child, which Pastor Sweet knew something of, but since he had so many other kids throughout the country, he decided to forfeit and allow Skeeter to be the father. When Skeeter was declared the father, he not only jumped for joy; this brother had a name already picked out. He also assumed that the unborn child would be a male. The real shocker was finding out that my nephew's name would be Hitler. Occasionally, Skeeter would look up historical information about past leaders and so happened to come across German history and thought the name had a heavenly ring to it. I tried to fight for my unborn nephew, but Skeeter and my sister insisted on that name! The next step was getting them married, and neither of them had money, so I was forced to once again deal with Pastor Sweet and set up a payment plan for them to wed. Can you believe that Pastor Sweet refused to marry them? He said that it was a conflict of interest since he already had fucked my sister several times. However, he'd gladly direct the couple to the pastor who taught and guided him while being locked up. A day later, we were in front of the preacher that Pastor Sweet suggested. Like Sweet, he also had a payment plan and was five times more expensive! As this preacher spoke the nuptials, his resemblance to Pastor Sweet was uncanny. Something didn't seem right, so I bum-rushed the pulpit and ripped off the preacher's blond wig. Wouldn't you know that it was Pastor Sweet in a disguise, pretending to be another preacher in order to charge more money. Since time was of the essence, I decided to be the bigger man and ignore the shenanigans of Sweet. You'd think that hardly anybody would attend my sister's wedding, but the turnout was miraculous, even with a $5 cover charge at the church door. When Sweet stated, "If there is anyone who sees fit that this couple shouldn't be married, speak now or forever hold your peace." After that announcement, all three hundred guests stood up, with written essays on why this freak show shouldn't continue. With every guest speaking their claim, we had a Guinness Book record of a wedding that lasted eleven hours! The wedding reception was BYOB, meaning "Bring your own burger." This fucking wedding was nearly putting me in the poor house, so a nigga had to lean on the guests for food! Luckily, Skeeter's mom brought some oatmeal, so the menu was a bit more diverse.

CHAPTER 15
The Stud

What is it about weddings that somehow brings the monogamy out of a brother? There were so many beautiful women at the reception, but only one truly caught my attention. Evidence would suggest that she was a lesbian or the more common word *stud* or *dike*. Her name even had a sexy ring to it, Hank. I and Hank talked for hours on the subject of homosexuality and how the both of us could get past this obstacle and possibly pursue a relationship. Most people have one shot at true love, so the both of us wasted very little time in arranging the wedding. Our ceremony was quick and to the point; we probably stayed in the courthouse no longer than five minutes. Hank and I were both so anxious to consummate our love, but that even proved to be difficult. I was Hank's first male lover, and the sight of a naked man put her in a state of panic. To put her at ease somewhat, I threw on a matching set of bra and panties just to bring some calmness to the situation. This seemed to get us up to the point of foreplay but nothing else. Eventually, she let her guard down, and we began to have natural sex like any other sane couple. Still, there was something wrong. Hank would come to bed with a flannel shirt on and hair around her face from not shaving daily. With her looking like this at bedtime hours, it was hard for a nigga to get aroused. I couldn't totally raise hell about her looking like a hot mess because this was her appearance before we met. Hank and I were compromising people, so when I asked her to place an open can of tuna between her legs at bedtime to mimic a vagina that truly yearned for a man, she said yes! I even demanded that she wear a thong but later changed my mind caused it looked like a Slim Jim going up her booty! As the months went on, our marriage seemed to get worse by the minute. Hank decided that seeing a marital counselor was a must in order for this shit to work. The counselor asked Hank about her gripes concerning the marriage. Her only complaint was that I left pubic hairs in the bathtub after showering. Our counselor saw that the problem was mostly with Hank; therefore, private sessions were scheduled for my wife only. For some reason, Hank seemed to think that our counselor was picking on her. After that, my wife refused further counseling then later filed for a divorce. I went into a deep depression about losing my wife. I had to be taken to the ER because of an overdose on cough syrup. Suicide consumed my thoughts nearly every minute! I had to have family members around me at all times just so that a nigga wouldn't jump off the roof! Eventually, I got it back together then decided to fight for my marriage! A month had gone by, and Hank was nowhere to be found. When she left me, I had an address, but when I drove past the house, it was condemned. Getting in contact with her family members was almost impossible! Apparently, she had threatened them at gunpoint to not say anything about her whereabouts. However, love makes you a detective, so I gathered my common sense and figured that she'd probably be hanging around the local gay joints. As I pulled up in front of the building, I could see Hank hugged up with some chick. Anger got a hold of me, so I rushed up in there like a black power movement and started beating her lover's ass! After the beat down, I dragged my wife out of there, made love to her, and assured her that the second time will be better, so I thought. Every morning, I would wake up slightly damp with a skin rash. There was also a foul smell that was associated with this strange moisture. Whenever I would do the laundry, I would notice that Hank's boxers were at the bottom of the hamper, covered with yellowish-brown stains. I came to find out that Hank was pissing the bed! This marriage was once again on the brink of failure. For better or worse was all I could think of. So the next day, I brought some diapers home and insisted that she wear them! We fought all night until she threw her hands up in the air and said, "NO MAN IS GONNA TELL ME WHAT TO DO, ONLY A WOMAN CAN!" This was the last I ever saw of Hank, and believe it or not, there will always be a special place for that evil bitch in my heart.

CHAPTER 16
Butter

A brother is now single, sexy, and free. Now who wants me? This was my new daily mantra. When you're out of the game for a while, the mack daddy gets dusty and rusty, so I had to psych myself up since I told all my ex-hoes to go to hell. My mom would always say to me, "Bitch, never burn your bridges," and now I am looking like Willie Lump Lump, all alone and shit. My ass was on the rebound, and the last thing I wanted to do is appear desperate. One day while rummaging through my neighbor's trashcan in a final attempt to determine the gender, this smooth, well-dressed sister named Butter drove by and hollered, "You got a nice ass." Her approach immediately got my attention 'cause in today's world, you hardly find women who are honest. Our first meeting was a short hi and good-bye due to her cell phone constantly ringing. It was no-brainer that the sister was self-employed by the way she spoke on the phone to her business associates. Every time her cell rung, Butter would begin the conversation with "Bitch, where is my money?" During our five-minute courtship, I heard her say this at least ten times. Even though we didn't speak long, she left me her business card with a questionnaire on the back concerning my suit and jacket sizes. Indeed, it was an odd business card, but when someone is feeling you and has an endless amount of cash, one doesn't ask a whole lot of questions! You just go with the flow. Our first date was at the food court in the mall. It just so happened that there was a clothing store near the court, so Butter pulled me by the ear, picked out a yellow suit, then ordered me to wear it. Next, she personally gave me a haircut then sprayed my entire body with air freshener. Afterward, Butter stuck the company phone in my back pocket then dropped me off at her friend's house while she ran a few errands. This friend was a creepy middle-aged woman who was wheelchair bound and with no legs. I thought this situation to be odd 'cause this old hag didn't speak. All she did was fondle my genitals for one whole hour. At first, I wanted to pull away, but there was no harm being done, so I let her have her jollies. Eventually, Butter came back and rushed my ass to the car. While in the ride, I noticed that the friend was paying Butter huge sums of money. When Butter returned to the car, she gave me $20 then said, "Good job, bitch." For once, I had a girl with money and power! No longer would a nigga have to worry about shut-off notices and child support. Still, I was on the rebound and very much vulnerable, which worried me 'cause I was beginning to think that Butter was pimping me. I finally decided that Butter was exercising way too much control over me when she demanded that I return to the old hag's house and run on the treadmill buck naked. When I refused her demand, she slapped then choked me until I blacked out! Whenever I refused her demand, the more violent this power-mad bitch got! Everyone would ask, "Why are you letting this woman abuse you so?" See, when you're heartbroken from a previous relationship, it can really damage your esteem. The shock of the hour came when I finally came out of my depression then realized Butter to be a pimp. When I told Butter no more, she replied, "I've invested a lot of money in your ass, and you ain't going nowhere, playa." As I tried to bounce, Butter grabbed a butter knife then stabbed me in the ass. I was now injured and without the ability to run! While I lay on the floor with a bleeding ass, Butter dragged me down to the basement, pulled off my clothes, turned the radio up to drown the hollering out, then tortured me for forty days and forty nights by cutting small incisions into my penis then pouring lemon juice on them. This abusive relationship went on for nearly six months until I went into hiding at Pastor Sweet's crib. Unfortunately, Butter found me and demanded my return from the pastor. Unbeknown to me, Butter was a former member of the pastor's church who occasionally, like me, sought counseling. This gave Sweet the edge in negotiating my freedom from this gangsta bitch, which he did so tactfully. Butter claimed that she still had at least five thousand invested in my ass, and losing my services would be financially catastrophic for her. Sweet agreed to pay her for the loss on the condition that I work off the debt by doing some odd jobs around the church. My first assignment came the following Sunday when Sweet asked me to dress up like an elderly man and sit in a wheelchair until I was called to the pulpit. As Sweet preached his sermon on miracles, he then pointed my way and demanded me to walk to the pulpit. As I slowly approached the pulpit, Sweet screamed, "IT'S A MIRACLE!" His now flourishing congregation was pouring out the dough as if the recession never happened. I was now a tool in Satan's garden, and crooked Sweet exploited me to the fullest. Sweet knew that my wheelchair routine was the biggest moneymaker his church ever saw, so he offered me a full-time job at $1,000 a week if I agreed to stay on well after the debt was paid, which was a strong hell to the no. After three months of this cartoon shit, Sweet was now reimbursed, and that meant my conscience could now be set free.

CHAPTER 17
Taking Him In

Ever have one of those days when you go to wipe your ass and a finger goes straight through the toilet paper? When days like this come about, one just knows that bad news is coming. My nephew, Hitler, was now ten years of age and having all sorts of problems. After he beat his gym teacher with a dog chain, Skeeter thought it be best for Hitler to stay with me since I am a miracle worker with kids. At first, I didn't want to take in that little hell spawn, but since he was the love child of my sister and my dearest friend, I just couldn't say "Fuck no!" Off the bat, I and Hitler had a falling-out. Evidently, Hitler believed that he could stay up as long as possible since I had the cable bill in his name. When I told him that bedtime was at eight, this little bitch grabbed a bat and began to smash up the furniture then threatened to keep on destroying shit if I didn't let him stay up and watch reruns of his favorite show, *Flavor of Love*. Immediately I got a hold of an extension cord, made him take off his clothes, and whipped his ass until the break of dawn! It seems as though the more I beat Hitler, the more he enjoyed it. Clearly, he was into pain and pleasure, so my disciplinary techniques had to change. Hitler carried a broken glass bottle for the purpose of cutting a classmate up, so for punishment, I took it away until the grades on his report card improved. Just like his father, Hitler could eat. Nothing was safe around him, not even hamster pellets! He would suck on them as though they were Tic Tacs. Eventually, I was able to obtain a food stamp card just so I could keep enough food in the house. Yet still that wasn't even enough. Things got to the point where I had to hide the food at my girlfriend's house in order to have something to eat for the next day. Finally, I took Hitler to a physician to see why on earth he was so greedy. I came to find out that Hitler had a tapeworm inside of him from eating raw bacon. Hitler was a member of my family, so that classified him as a freak. I began to suspect that early puberty was setting in because all my porno flicks were missing! Also, I noticed that Hitler was taking two-hour showers. Clearly, this was a sign of masturbation, so I decided to teach him the birds and the bees by making him watch two monkeys have sex on the TV show *Animal Kingdom*. Can't say that he caught on to the reasoning behind me making him watch this program, but now every day, with the exceptions of weekends, he'd go to the zoo then climb into the gorilla cage with no clothes on. With early puberty, there are also random erections! Hitler was terrified of the dark. Maybe because Skeeter and my sister kept the lights out at their crib? See, they never made enough money to keep the lights on. So most nights, he slept with me, even if I had a naked woman in the bed. One night, I felt something poking me, almost like a knife in my back. At first, I thought a spring from my mattress had come out. But then I remembered me sleeping on the floor 'cause I couldn't afford a bed. After much investigation into this matter, my nephew's little pecker had now come of age! I thought that I would turn out to be the proud uncle of a child who was sleeping with his fifth-grade teacher, but that dream was shot to hell, knowing how retarded Hitler was. Still, he was going through puberty, which is the threshold for an aspiring freak, so it was my obligation to guide him through. Even though Skeeter was his daddy, there was no way in hell that I was going to let Hitler turn out like him. In grade school, Skeeter was a social reject. I was going to turn Hitler into a grade school pimp—respectfully, of course! I made him wear a white three-piece suit to class daily and told him that I'd fuck him up if he got it dirty at recess. Shit, a brother paid $300 for that suit, so in no way could I allow him to be irresponsible in getting it dirty. Next I told him to send at least twelve girls a love letter with a dollar in it. Hitler had no money; therefore, I had to loan the money to him under the condition that he pay me back in five years, when old enough to get a summer job. I was trying to build a support system for Hitler in the form of a harem. Hitler needed all the support that he could get, being that he was dumb as hell. I just wanted him to be promoted to the sixth grade, and doing so required that he pass math. Just like I knew, his harem came to his aid by doing his homework for him. *Now that is what I call pimp potential!*

CHAPTER 18
Shabba

With a failed marriage and an existence filled with crazy people, I had personally deemed my life as a disaster. The only person, or should I say thing, to give me peace was my cat, Shabba. He was the only one that didn't demand sex from me while lying in bed. All he required was beer and bologna in his food dish daily. Shabba didn't care to go out at night like most cats. Instead he'd rather sleep on my ass under my pajamas in the late hours of the night. As I said earlier, Shabba didn't demand sex, but I felt that he was leaning toward the moment by the erotic twitch of his whiskers. Sleeping with Shabba was peaceful until about 3:00 a.m. Under my pajamas, he would bury his face in between my booty cheeks—I guess for comfort and relaxation. Of course, this kept me up, yet still I felt appreciated. People say that dogs are man's best friend, but I will repudiate that in a heartbeat! Daily I would strap my belt around Shabba's neck then walk him around the neighborhood. With every ten steps, I nearly strangled Shabba, so loosening the buckle at the ninth step was critical to his survival. One day, I got so involved with looking at this big-booty sister that I lost focus. Below me was Shabba lying unconscious from strangulation. Quickly a brother seized the moment and began CPR on my cat. People walked by and gasped as though a woman was breast-feeding her child in the middle of a football stadium. Such ignorance! I was only trying to save my cat from the grim reaper, and these assholes had something to say? This wasn't the first time of almost killing Shabba, so I wasn't worried about him coming out of a near-death experience. He has done it before and will do it again! Shabba has defied all odds by being on his twelfth life. When Shabba finally came back to consciousness, our relationship changed. One night, I brought a young lady home from the bar straight to the bedroom. This girl wanted me and wasted no time in unzipping my pants. Being that it was pitch-black, I couldn't quite see what she was doing, but the intensity of the moment kept me hard as a rock! As this woman sucked away on my johnson, there was no feeling at all. At first, I thought the sexual excitement was having an adverse affect on me, therefore paralyzing my pecker! Twenty minutes had now gone by and still no feeling from the oral sex. This shit was racking my brain, so I lit a match to see what was going the hell on. I came to find out that this silly bitch was sucking on my cat's tail. Since I'm always a gentlemen, I held the door open then told her to never come the fuck back! Shabba was now cock blocking me, which made him my enemy! I loved Shabba with all my heart, so killing him wasn't going to be easy. My plan was to skin him then make a sweatband out of his fur. Shabba sensed that I had ill feelings toward him, so he avoided me for about a week. One night, as he was taking a shit in his litter box, I snuck up on him with a knife. Before I could end his existence, he caught wind to what I was doing and ran into my closet. I then locked the door and began taunting him with evil words like *bad pussy*, *rotten pussy*, and *stank pussy*. As I hurled insults, Shabba's meows were more like calls for help. As the night moved forward, I then decided it was about time to open the closet door and kill my pussy! When the door opened, Shabba zoomed out that motherfucker like a rocket then shot out the front door. Last I heard, he was running toward Chinatown. His chances of survival were probably better with me!

CHAPTER 19
Hitlers Graduation

When we put our lives under a microscope, there is a realization that we're all fucked up, so proud moments come along and give us hope! My whole family is now attending Hitler's grade school graduation, and for some unknown reason, everybody is staring at us. Maybe because Uncle Eric just got arrested for back child support in the school's auditorium. Or was it because Aunt Brenda decided to take off her bra in front of everybody then placed it in the lap of the dude sitting next to her? Whatever the reason was, staring is so impolite and sends the wrong signals. I made my family promise to not come drunk in order to keep shit calm. If I had not done that, all those who stared would've gotten fucked up with a capital *F*. It seemed like forever waiting on Hitler to walk the stage. My family was getting impatient 'cause they kept throwing bottles and booing all the other kids who walked the stage. Security had to step in and break up a fight between my sister and a lady in the audience. This pissed me off because all my sister did was call some kid a pussy while he accepted his diploma. The moment of truth had now arrived! Hitler pimp-strutted across the stage with a pink cap and gown on, courtesy of me. This proud moment brought tears to our eyes. As the principal handed Hitler his certificate of achievement, Pastor Sweet stormed onstage and declared Hitler to be his son. We were now locked in a custody battle, and the only way to solve it is to determine who really fucked my sister first. My family pulled out their knives then demanded that all three hundred people leave the auditorium so that we could have some family time and resolve this issue. Pastor Sweet felt that since he was getting older, there needed to be an heir to his congregation and shady businesses. The pastor had at least fifty kids and counting, but not one showed any promise in the event if he should pass. After a long game of rock, paper, and scissors to determine paternity, Skeeter was again declared the boy's daddy! Pastor Sweet forfeited his right long ago, and now he wants to come back and play daddy? It just doesn't work like that. With all the confusion in the auditorium, I almost forgot Hitler's graduation gift. I and the entire family spent hours trying to figure out the appropriate gift for a special needs case such as my nephew. After everything was said and done, we got him an Etch A Sketch and told him it was a tablet. And guess what? He believed it.

CHAPTER 20
The Incarceration Of Sweet

Pastor Sweet is now a local TV evangelist with about five thousand in his congregation. The one-time street hustler, who robbed convenience stores for a living, now was residing in a deluxe apartment on the south side of York, Pennsylvania. With his boost in popularity, he now could sit at home with three buck-naked honeys and send his sermons to all in his congregation through text messages. Still, every now and then, he would make a guest appearance for Sunday service. Members of the church began to question where their money was going since they still had to congregate in his backyard. Even though the church was being televised, members felt embarrassed about being in a holy place with a ceiling made out of garbage bags. One day the members cornered the church secretary then demanded that he show them the books. As the members reviewed the notebook written in crayon, they discovered that the church was in bankruptcy from failed business ventures. Apparently, Sweet had started a chain of strip clubs called Righteous Boobs that fell through because his appointed deacon over business affairs embezzled all the money. They also found monetary gifts to his various parole officers. Sweet had so much foul shit on him that he was forced to pay the officers substantial monies in order to keep himself free. Today, Pastor Sweet has started a prison-ministry outreach program as an inmate at a Pennsylvania correction facility. He is serving a six-year sentence for misappropriations of church funds. In jail, he has a decent following, and all he requires at Sunday service is that his followers put packs of cigarettes in the collection plate.

CHAPTER 21
Lost In The Sauce..

Skeeter and my sister will forever have an on-and-off relationship 'cause nobody in their right mind wants either of them, so they'll be eternally stuck together. Four to five times a year, Skeeter has to be hospitalized for continual odd behavior. As I repeatedly stated before, Skeeter is the nicest person you'll ever want to know. His kindness stretches out to all regardless of race, nationality, or affiliation. Just yesterday, he even left the night-light on for potential burglars. In his own mind, Skeeter believes that he is a celebrity around the hood. So whenever his psychiatrist would ask him to lie on the couch, he assumed it was an interview instead of an evaluation. Matter of fact, he and my sister have now moved up in the world. Instead of living in a one-bedroom, one-bath Section 8 house, they're now living in a four-bedroom, two-bath Section 8 house. It is so hard being around both of them now 'cause their noses are stuck so far in the air that they can't smell their own mouthwash! Still, I love them immensely. May the both of them live happily never after!

CHAPTER 22
Who's Baby??

As for me, I have gotten a little wiser. My days of womanizing are finally over! I have accepted my role as a true leader in the black community and not someone who is just going through the motions. I have decided that my big white woman fetish is something that I just cannot ignore, so I decided to marry again and take one as a wife. Every now and then, she tries to put me out for beating her ass. Hey, I married an overweight lover and don't want her large ass to ever change, so I refuse to let her stay on a diet. Aside from our marital problems, I have grown to love her unconditionally. Every time her big ass eats applesauce at dinnertime, the shit turns me on. Truly, there is a Misses for every mister. I was beginning to believe that I would never find a true compatible mate. Right now, I am in the delivery room, waiting for my son to be born. This big-ass white woman is yelling and screaming like someone is murdering her! It ain't that I'm ignorant. I know all too well the discomforts of childbirth. When my son finally arrived, my wife pulled out a photograph, looked at it, then looked at me. My wife said, "Baby, don't get mad, but I have been visiting the correctional facility in Pennsylvania for religious counseling, and my stays have turned into conjugal visits, and you are now the proud father of Pastor Sweet's son." What the *fuck!*